A Bike for Big-Ears

Collins

It was a sunny morning in Toy Town…

Noddy was driving carefully, as usual. But
on this particular day he had a very tricky
passenger in his car.

"Don't put me off while I'm driving," he told
Clockwork Clown, "or we'll have a crash."

"Who, me? I wouldn't dream of it, Noddy,"
grinned Clockwork Clown.

Noddy stopped at the road junction just outside
Toy Town.

Ting-a-ling-a-ling! Big-Ears rang his bell as he
cycled past.

"Big-Ears must be going into Toy Town to buy
something at Dinah Doll's stall," said Noddy.

Clockwork Clown wasn't listening. With a grin, he took out a shiny, red balloon and – BANG! – he popped it! It gave Noddy a real fright.

"Aghh!" he yelled and, by mistake, he put his foot down on the accelerator. Before he knew what had happened, the car was skidding crazily through the streets of Toy Town.

Noddy struggled to stop his car. "Phew! That wasn't very nice," he gasped.

But just as Noddy turned to ask Clockwork Clown why he'd played such a silly trick, the clown leaped up and did a somersault over the windscreen.

"Thanks for the ride, Noddy!" he grinned.

Noddy was very upset. He'd almost had a crash thanks to that balloon!

"I *do* drive carefully," he said to himself as he drove on, "but it's difficult with clowns like that in the car. I'm a *good* driver…"

CRRUNNNCH!

"Uh-oh! I've hit something!" cried poor Noddy.

"Oh, no!" groaned Big-Ears, who had been
talking to Dinah Doll. "My beautiful bike!
You've crushed it!"

"I'm so sorry, Big-Ears! I'm really, really
sorry!" cried Noddy.

"They don't make bikes like that any more,"
moaned Big-Ears, looking at his smashed bike.
    "Don't worry, Big-Ears," said Noddy. "I'll take
it to Mr Sparks. He'll know what to do."
    "Noddy's right, Big-Ears," said Dinah Doll.
"If anyone can fix it, Mr Sparks can."

Noddy's face lit up. "And he could add some new things," he said. "A big horn, or flashing lights, or…"

"No horns. No flashing lights," said Big-Ears, firmly.

"But Big-Ears…" cried Noddy.

"No, Noddy. I don't want anything new. My bike was perfect just as it was."

"Oh, all right," said Noddy.

Noddy took Big-Ears' bike to the Toy Town garage.

"Can you fix it, Mr Sparks?" he asked.

"Of course, Noddy, I'll make it as good as new."

"I bet you could make it even better!" said
Noddy. "But Big-Ears wants his old bike back
just as it was."

"Some people don't like change," said Mr Sparks.

"I feel bad about wrecking his bike, Mr Sparks," said Noddy. "Is there any way you could make it better than it was?"

"Hmm," said Mr Sparks. "Ah-ha, I do have an idea, Noddy. I could fit Big-Ears' bike with a motor."

"Oh, *yes*, Mr Sparks!" Noddy was thrilled. "A motor would make his bike much more fun."

"Can you hide the motor in this basket?"
Noddy asked. "Then Big-Ears'll get a real
surprise when he starts pedalling."

"Fitting a motor in a basket is quite a
challenge," said Mr Sparks, "...but I like it!"
And he rolled up his sleeves and got started.

"Thundering toadstools! It's ALIVE!" cried poor Big-Ears as his pedalling kick-started the motor-in-a-basket.

"Aaghh!" he shrieked as the bike roared away. "Watch out, Noddy. I can't stop! HELP!"

Big-Ears tried his best to steer, but his bike was going too fast. It swerved around Noddy and zoomed off down the road towards Toy Town, with Big-Ears clinging on for dear life.

Noddy jumped into his little car and tore after Big-Ears.

"Quick, little car, we've got to rescue Big-Ears!"
cried Noddy, chasing after the runaway bike.
  As Noddy raced along, he shouted, "Slow
down, Big-Ears!"
  "I caaaaaaan't!" yelled Big-Ears.

Big-Ears, on the runaway bike, hurtled past Clockwork Clown.

Then Noddy whizzed by.

"Whooahh!" Clockwork Clown was whirled round by the whoosh of air from the car.

"Oops! Sorry!" yelled Noddy. "Can't stop!"

"Any minute now," cried Noddy in a panic, "we'll be in the middle of Toy Town's busy streets!"

Ting-a-ling-a-ling! Big-Ears rang his bell madly, warning everyone to get out of his way.

"Sorry!" he shouted as he shot past Mr Wobbly Man and sent him spinning across the road.

"Look out! Coming through!" Big-Ears yelled as he bounced off a rubbish bin, ran over a little tree, then whizzed past Clockwork Mouse, Mr Jumbo, Dinah Doll and Tessie Bear.

"Looks like Mr Sparks got that bike working a little *too* well," said Dinah Doll.

At top speed, Big-Ears roared straight into Mr Sparks' open garage.

CRASH! BANG! BUMP! THUMP! CRUNCH!

Tools, bits and pieces of cars and bikes flew through the air as Big-Ears smashed into the workshop – and out again.

"Help!" wailed Big Ears. "I can't hold on much longer!"

Noddy had to do something – and fast!

He drove up behind his old friend, yelling, "When I say, 'Now!' Big-Ears, jump into my car!"

"OK!" Big-Ears gasped. "Just get me off this thing!"

It wasn't easy to drive alongside the runaway
bike, but Noddy managed it.
   "Ready… NOW!" he shouted.

Big-Ears leaped off his bike — and into
Noddy's car.

   He was safe at last, thanks to Noddy's brave
and clever driving. His bike zoomed straight into
a wall. KERRUNCH!

   Big-Ears' bike was smashed again. But at least
the motor-in-a-basket had finally stopped.

"I'm sorry, Big-Ears. I wanted to make your bike better. So I asked Mr Sparks to put a motor on it."

"So I see, Noddy," said Big-Ears. "Next time you want to help someone, do what they ask for, not what you think is best for them!"

"I will," said Noddy. "I'll ask Mr Sparks to mend your bike just the way you like it."

Then Noddy grinned. "Are you *sure* you don't want any flashing lights, Big-Ears?" he asked.

"You funny little Noddy," said Big-Ears. "You know I don't."

And they both laughed until the bell on Noddy's hat jingled.

First published in Great Britain by HarperCollins Publishers Ltd in 2002

5 7 9 10 8 6

This edition published by HarperCollins Children's Books
HarperCollins Children's Books is a division of HarperCollins Publishers Ltd.

ISBN: 0 00 715105 5

Printed and bound by Printing Express Ltd., Hong Kong

make way for
NODDY ™

Do-It-Yourself Noddy
ISBN 0 00 712241 1

Noddy Goes Shopping
ISBN 0 00 712242 X

Collect them all!

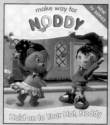

Hold on to your Hat, Noddy
ISBN 0 00 712243 8

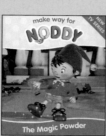

The Magic Powder
ISBN 0 00 715101 2

Noddy and the Magic Bagpipes
ISBN 0 00 712366 3

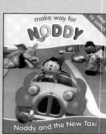

Noddy and the New Taxi
ISBN 0 00 712239 X

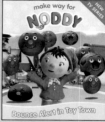

Bounce Alert in Toy Town
ISBN 0 00 715103 9

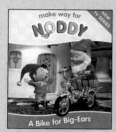

A Bike for Big-Ears
ISBN 0 00 715105 5

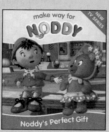

Noddy's Perfect Gift
ISBN 0 00 712365 5

Noddy's Special Treat
ISBN 0 00 712362 0

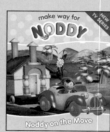

Noddy on the Move
ISBN 0 00 715678 2

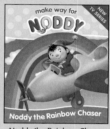

Noddy the Rainbow Chaser
ISBN 0 00 715677 4

**And send off for your free Noddy poster (rrp £3.99).
Simply collect 4 tokens and complete the coupon below.**

✂ -

TOKEN

Name: _____

Address: _____

_____

_____

e-mail: _____

❏ Tick here if you do wish to receive further information about children's books.

Send coupon to: **Noddy Poster Offer, PO Box 142, Horsham, RH13 5FJ**

Terms and conditions: proof of sending cannot be considered proof of receipt. Not redeemable for cash. 28 days delivery. Offer open to UK residents only.

UNIVERSAL

Make Way for Noddy videos now available at all good retailers